Este libro pertenece a:

This book belongs to:

....

Brimax Publishing
415 Jackson St, San Francisco
CA 94111 USA
www.brimax.com.au

Illustrated by Sue Lisansky
Copyright © Brimax Publishing, 2006
Printed in China (August 2011) 10 9 8 7 6

La Cenicienta · Cinderella

Ilustrado por • Illustrated by
Sue Lisansky

La Cenicienta vivía en una gran casa con sus dos feas hermanastra
Ellas le hacían hacer todo el trabajo. Las dos hermanastras pasaban
mucho tiempo cada día intentando verse bonitas.

Un día, llego una carta invitando a las dos hermanastras a un gran
baile en el palacio real.

"¿Puedo yo ir también?," preguntó la Cenicienta.

"No," respondieron sus hermanastras. "Tú debes ayudarnos a
alistarnos."

Cinderella lived in a big house with her two ugly stepsisters. They made her do all the work. The two stepsisters spent a lot of time each day trying to make themselves look pretty.

One day, a letter arrived inviting the two stepsisters to a grand ball at the king's palace.

"Can I come too?" asked Cinderella.

"No," said her stepsisters. "You must help us get ready."

La pobre Cenicienta vio como sus hermanastras se iban al baile con sus bellos vestidos. Ella se sentó con su sucio y estropeado vestido y lloró.

"Si solo pudiera ir yo también," dijo ella.

"Tú irás al baile," dijo una voz detrás de ella. La Cenicienta saltó sobresaltada.

"¿Quién eres tú?," preguntó la Cenicienta.

"Yo soy tu hada madrina," dijo la mujer.

Poor Cinderella watched as her stepsisters left for the ball in their beautiful gowns. She sat in her dirty, ragged dress and cried.

"If only I could go too," she said.

"You shall go to the ball," said a voice behind her. It made Cinderella jump.

"Who are you?" asked Cinderella.

"I am your fairy godmother," said the lady.

"Tráeme una calabaza, cuatro ratones blancos y tres lagartos verdes," dijo la hada madrina. La Cenicienta corrió a buscar todas esas cosas.

Con un golpe de su varita, ella transformó por arte de magia la calabaza en un carruaje. Los ratones y los lagartos se convirtieron en cuatro caballos blancos y tres cocheros.

"Bring me a pumpkin, four white mice, and three green lizards," said the fairy godmother. Cinderella ran to find all these things.

With a wave of her wand, she magically turned the pumpkin into a coach. The mice and lizards were turned into four white horses and three coachmen.

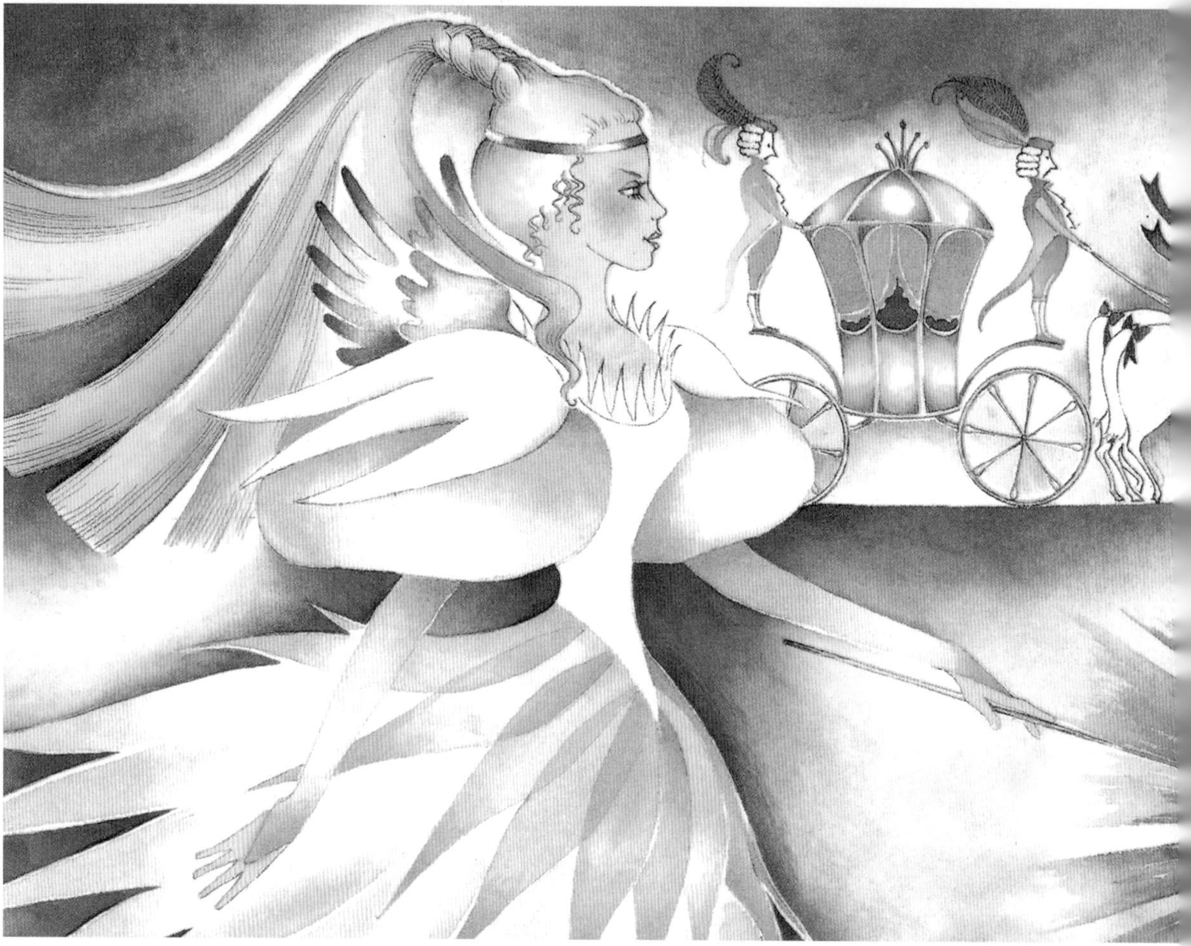

La Cenicienta no podía creer lo que veían sus ojos.

"¿Pero qué puedo vestir?," Ella preguntó con tristeza. "Yo solo tengo este viejo y estropeado vestido."

La buena hada madrina agitó su varita de nuevo y transformó sus viejos y estropeados harapos en un nuevo y hermoso vestido. Ella tenía unos delicados y pequeños zapatos en sus pies.

Cinderella could not believe her eyes.

"But what can I wear?" she asked, sadly. "I only have these old rags."

The fairy godmother waved her wand again and Cinderella's old rags turned into a pretty new dress. She had dainty little shoes on her feet.

"Ahora puedes ir al baile," dijo el hada madrina. "Pero la magia desaparecerá a la media noche."

"Gracias buena hada madrina," dijo la Cenicienta.

La Cenicienta se fue al baile. Nadie sabía quién era ella. El príncipe bailó con la bella desconocida toda la noche.

"Now you can go to the ball," said the fairy godmother. "But the magic ends at midnight."

"Thank you fairy godmother," said Cinderella.

Cinderella arrived at the ball. No one knew who she was. The prince danced with the pretty stranger all night long.

La Cenicienta estaba tan feliz que se olvidó de la hora. Entonces el reloj dio las doce.

"Debo irme," lloraba la Cenicienta, mientras se alejaba corriendo.

"¡Deténte!," lloró el príncipe. "¡No te vayas!"

La Cenicienta bajó corriendo las escaleras del palacio y uno de sus zapatos se le salió.

Cinderella was so happy that she forgot the time. Then the clock struck twelve.

"I must go," cried Cinderella, as she ran away.

"Stop!" cried the prince. "Do not go!"

Cinderella ran down the palace steps and one of her shoes fell off.

La magia se acabó y el carruaje volvió a ser una calabaza. Los caballos y los cocheros se convirtieron en los ratones blancos y los lagartos verdes.

El príncipe encontró el zapato de la Cenicienta.

"Yo debo encontrar a la joven que perdió este zapato," dijo el príncipe. "Ella será mi esposa."

The magic ended and the coach turned back into a pumpkin.
The horses and coachmen turned back into white mice and lizards.
   The prince found Cinderella's shoe.
   "I must find the girl who can wear this shoe," he said. "She will be
my bride."

El príncipe buscó por todas partes para encontrar a la dueña del zapato. El zapato no le venía bien a nadie. Al final, llegó a la casa de la Cenicienta.

La primera hermanastra se probó el zapato. Su pie era demasiado largo. La segunda hermanastra se probó el zapato entonces. Pero su pie era muy ancho.

The prince looked everywhere to find the shoe's owner. The shoe fit no one. At last, he came to Cinderella's house.

The first stepsister tried the shoe. Her foot was too long. The second stepsister tried the shoe. Her foot was too wide.

"¿Hay alguien ahí?," preguntó el príncipe.

La Cenicienta salió y se lo probó también. El zapato le venía perfecto.

Sus hermanastras estaban muy enojadas, pero el príncipe estaba muy feliz. Él y la Cenicienta se casaron y ellos vivieron felices por siempre.

"Is there anyone else?" asked the prince.

Cinderella came out and tried on the shoe. It fit perfectly.

Her stepsisters were very angry but the prince was very happy.

He and Cinderella were married and they lived happily ever after.

Nota para los padres

La colección *Mi primer cuento de hadas*, está diseñada especialmente para ayudar a mejorar el vocabulario y la comprensión lectora de los niños. Las siguientes actividades, le ayudarán a comentar el cuento con sus hijos, y hará la experiencia de leer más placentera.

Note to Parents

The *First Fairy Tales* series is specially designed to help improve your child's literacy and reading comprehension. The following activities will help you discuss the story with your child, and will make the experience of reading more pleasurable.

Aquí hay algunas palabras claves del cuento. ¿Puedes leerlas?

Here are some key words in the story. Can you read them?

el príncipe / prince

el zapato / shoe

la carta / letter

el baile / ball

el carruaje / coach

el vestido / dress

el palacio / palace

la hada / fairy

la calabaza / pumpkin

la hermana / sister

el ratón / mice

¿Cuánto puedes recordar de la historia?

¿Por qué la Cenicienta no puede ir al baile?

¿Qué le pide el hada madrina a la Cenicienta?

¿Qué viste la Cenicienta para el baile?

¿Con quién baila la Cenicienta en el baile?

¿A qué hora desaparece el hechizo del hada madrina?

¿Qué pierde la Cenicienta al irse del baile?

¿Cómo encuentra el príncipe a la Cenicienta?

How much of the story can you remember?

Why can't Cinderella go to the ball?

What does the fairy godmother ask Cinderella to get?

What does Cinderella wear to the ball?

Who does Cinderella dance with at the ball?

What time does the fairy godmother's magic end?

What does Cinderella lose as she leaves the ball?

How does the prince find Cinderella?

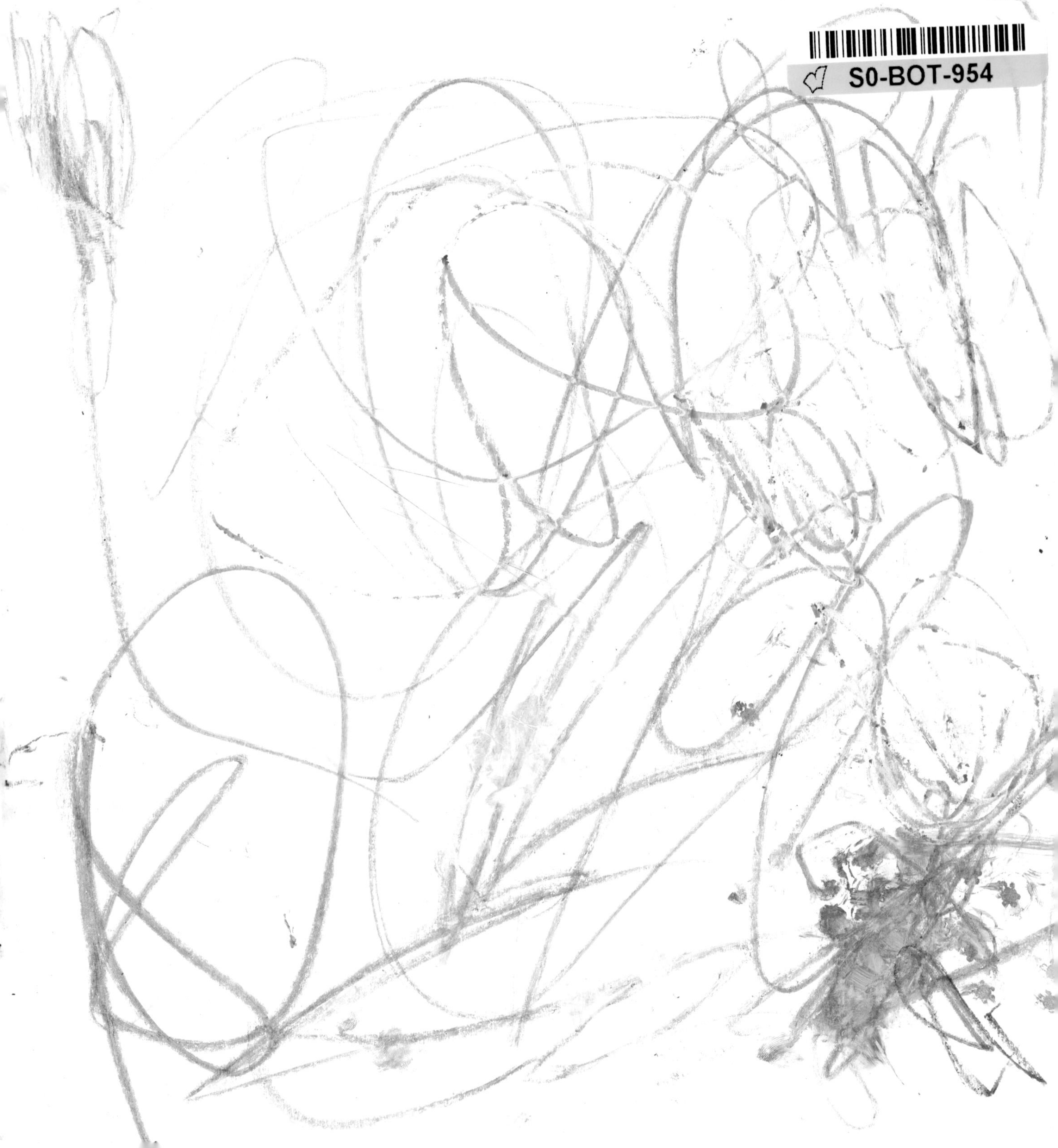

Lucky the Penguin

Lucky

Lucky

lucky the penguin

Lucky

Luku the Penuuin

Lucky

penguin

Lucky

Lucky

Lucky

LUCKY

Lucky the Penguin

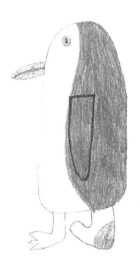

To Teddy, Sara, Benny, Myla, Wesley,
Jacob & Sophia – with love.
KBW

Story and Paintings by Karen B. Winnick
Text and Illustrations © 2016 by Karen B. Winnick
All Rights Reserved

Published by the
Santa Barbara Zoological Gardens
500 Niños Drive
Santa Barbara, California 93103
Printed in China

US Cataloging-in-Publication Data
(Library of Congress Standards)

Winnick, Karen B.
How Lucky Got His Shoe / by Karen B. Winnick – 1st Edition
[32] p. – col. Ill.; cm.
Summary: Lucky, a Humboldt penguin born with a deformed foot
at the Santa Barbara Zoo, gets his own shoe to help him walk and swim.
ISBN 9780984167814

Library of Congress Control Number 2016945716
First Edition, 2016
Layout Design: RosesRoad.com
Santa Barbara Zoo Advisor: Ross Reed Beardsley

How Lucky Got His Shoe

Karen B. Winnick

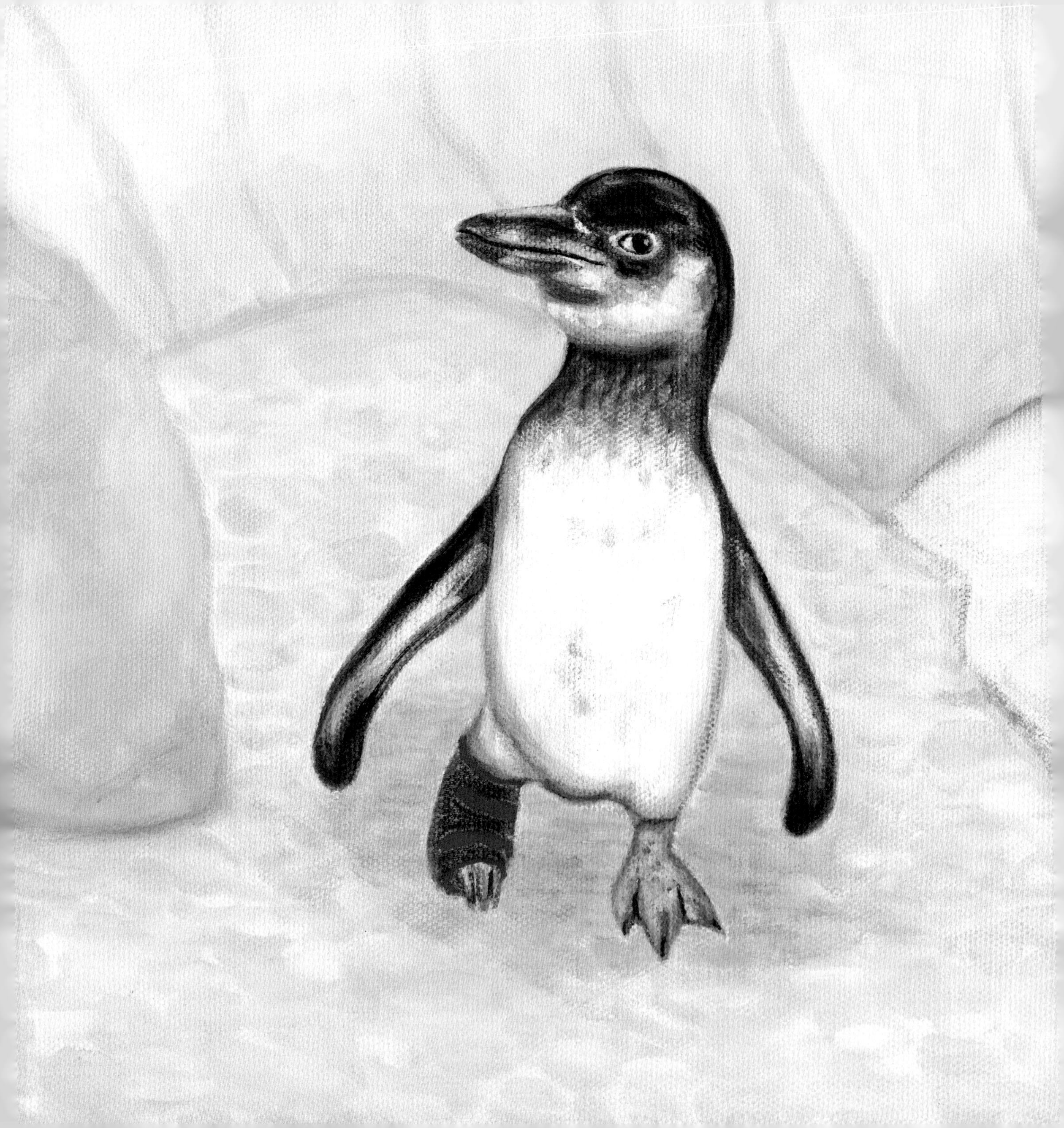

At the Santa Barbara Zoo, Lucky, a Humboldt penguin, waddles around the yard, hops up and down the rocks, swims in the pool and makes funny noises like all other penguins in the colony.

But there is something different about Lucky.

He is the only penguin at the Santa Barbara Zoo, maybe in the whole world, who wears a shoe.

Here's how Lucky got his shoe...

A baby Humboldt penguin was going to hatch at the Santa Barbara Zoo! His parents were taking turns warming the egg.

Rachel, the penguin keeper, was watching closely, checking underneath the parents in their burrow several times a day.

Early in the morning on April 15, 2010,
Rachel arrived at the Zoo and hurried to check.

She saw a chick covered in soft gray down feathers. He weighed a little more than three ounces. He was half the size of Rachel's hand.

Everyone was excited because each hatchling was important. Humboldt penguins are vulnerable in their native Peru.

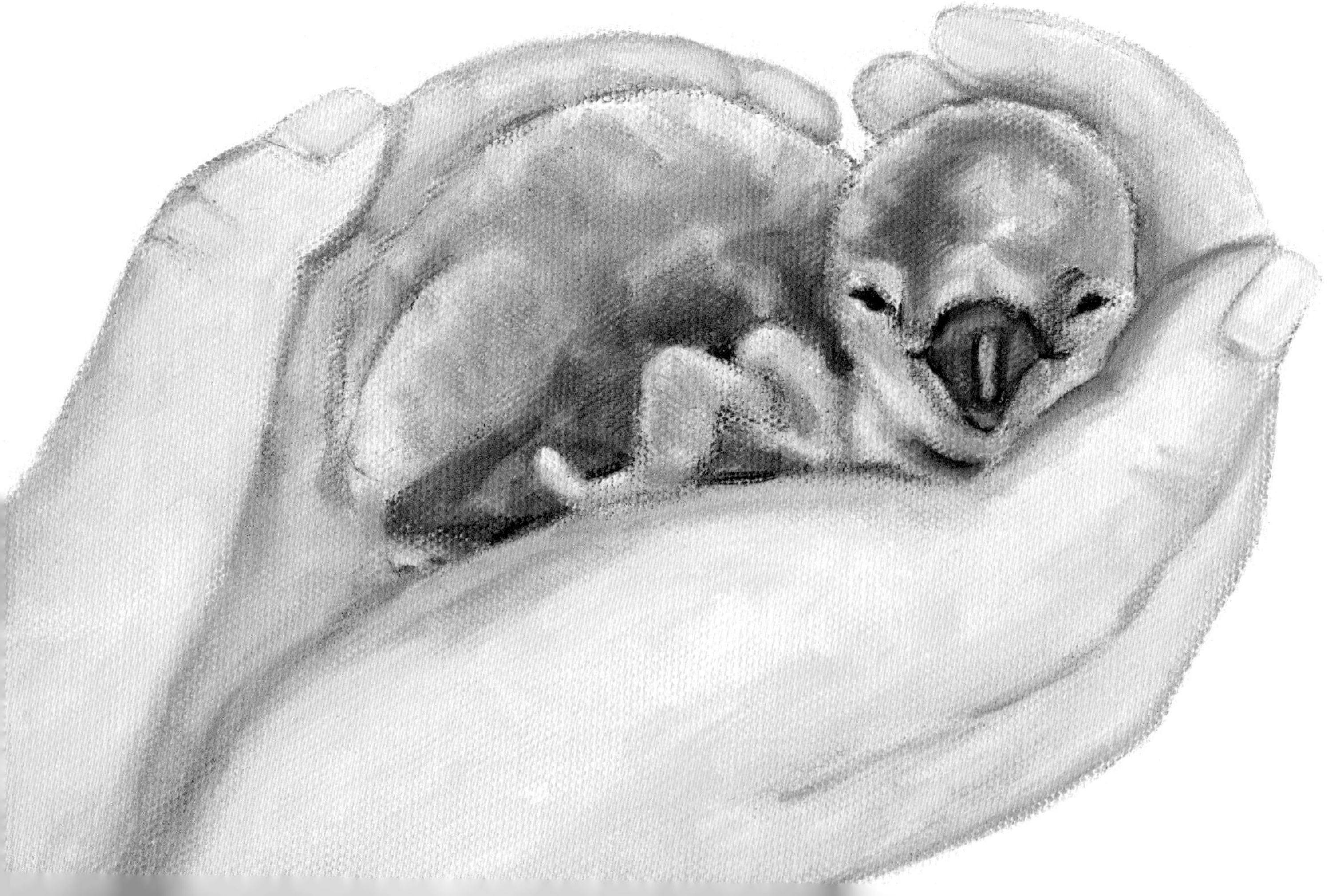

Rachel fed fish to the parents. Each one took turns coughing up their half-digested fish. They pushed it into the mouth of the hungry chick. The baby penguin ate and ate. He grew and grew.

Coarse waterproof feathers began to appear on his wings. They soon covered the rest of his body. The baby penguin was ready to walk out of his burrow, jump into the water and swim.

But when the chick walked, he dragged his right foot in an unsteady shuffle.

What was wrong, Rachel wondered?

Veterinarians took X-rays. "He doesn't appear
to have an injury," said one doctor.

"The chick's foot is not developing normally," said another.

The baby penguin continued to drag his foot along the ground. His skin became scraped. The doctors and zookeepers padded and wrapped his foot to protect it. But it didn't help.

They tried putting a splint on his foot. Rachel took it off
when he went swimming and put it back on when he
came out. Because he limped, she carried him to the water.
Later she needed to help him back out.

The penguin chick's foot grew worse. More sores developed. They became infected. Then, he couldn't swim at all.

Rachel and the others had to find some way to help him. His life depended on it.

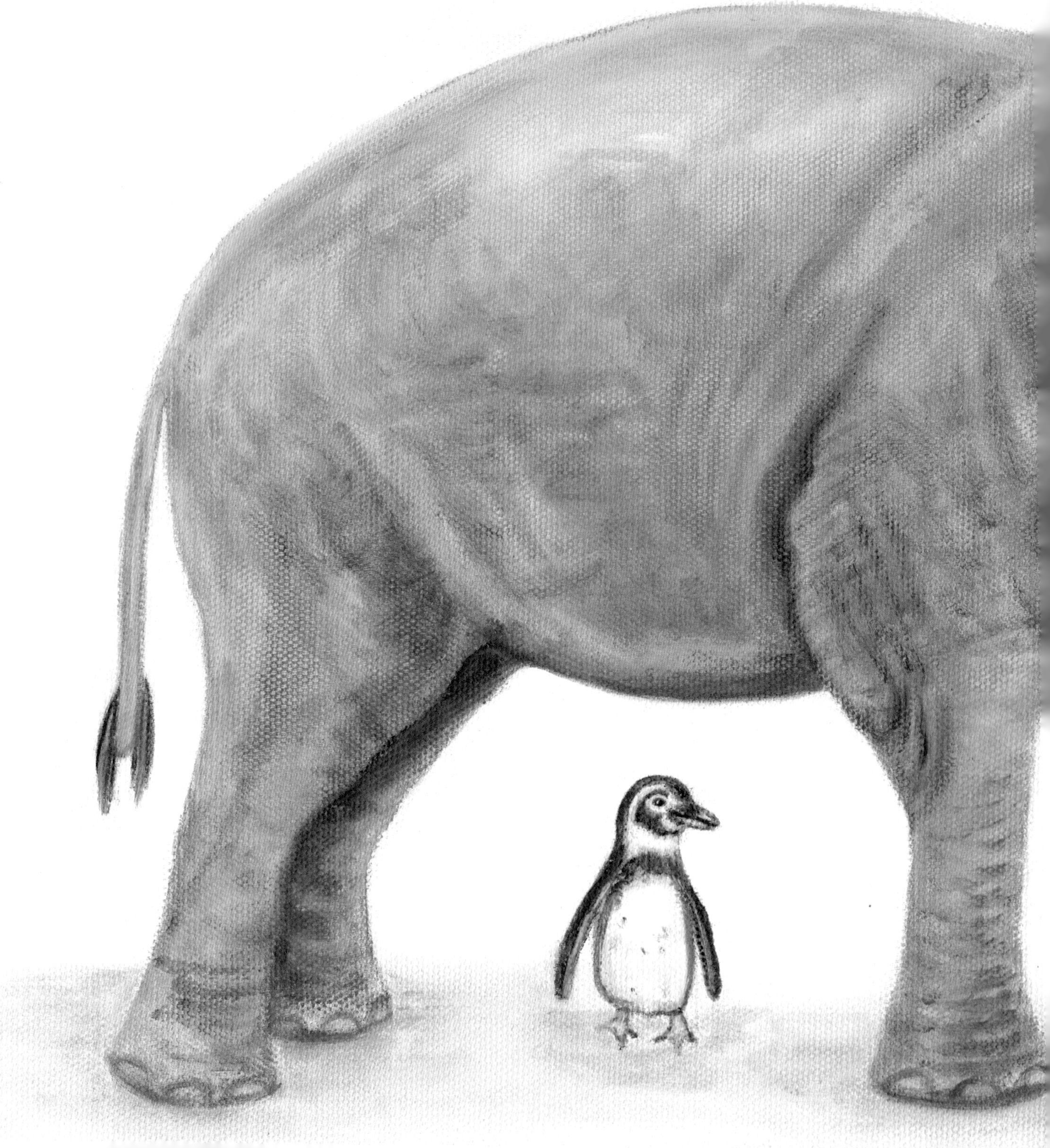

"A protective shoe was once made for an elephant with foot problems," remembered one zookeeper.

"A protective shoe might work," said Rachel. "If a shoe could be made for a big elephant, someone must be able to make a shoe for a little penguin."

A company called Teva was right in Santa Barbara. They made specialized shoes for "in, on and around the water."

Their design team agreed to help. They came out to the Zoo and observed the way the baby penguin limped. They studied his foot, how he dragged it and put pressure on his joint. While Rachel held him, they measured his foot and then made a mold of it.

"We'll make a perfect shoe for this lucky little bird," said one of the people from Teva.

"That's a perfect name!" said Rachel. "From now on that's what we'll call him. Lucky is lucky because we all care so much about him."

Teva made many drawings and models. They tried different materials. Finally they made a small hard shoe to hold his foot firmly in a natural position.

They came back to the Zoo
and fit it on Lucky's foot.

Lucky held his foot up.
He refused to walk.

"We need to come up with something that works better," said one Teva designer.

"But what?" another asked.

They experimented with more materials and different shapes and styles.

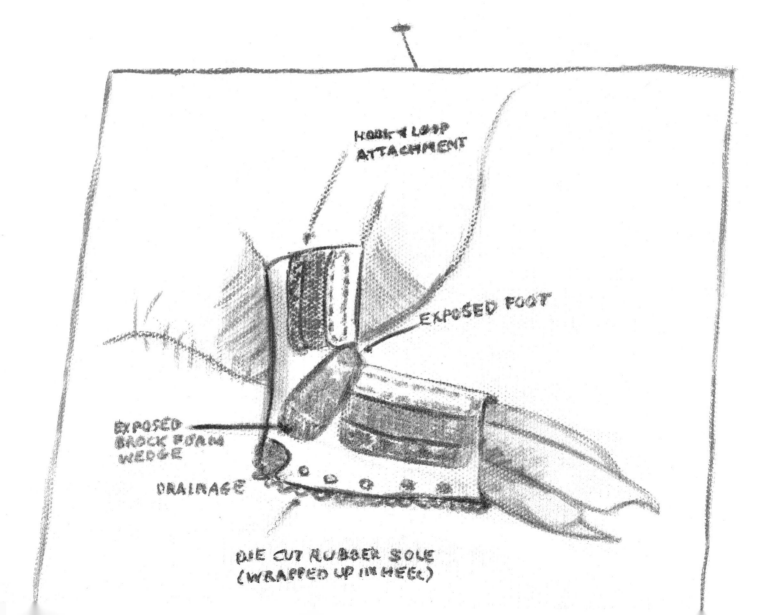

HOOK & LOOP ATTACHMENT

EXPOSED FOOT

EXPOSED BLOCK FOAM WEDGE

DRAINAGE

DIE CUT RUBBER SOLE (WRAPPED UP IN HEEL)

Weeks later they brought a new hand-sewn shoe for Lucky. It was soft and cushioned and made of a special new waterproof material that dried quickly.

Carefully they fit the shoe on Lucky's foot and secured it with the strap.

Lucky took a step...then another... and another....

and then...

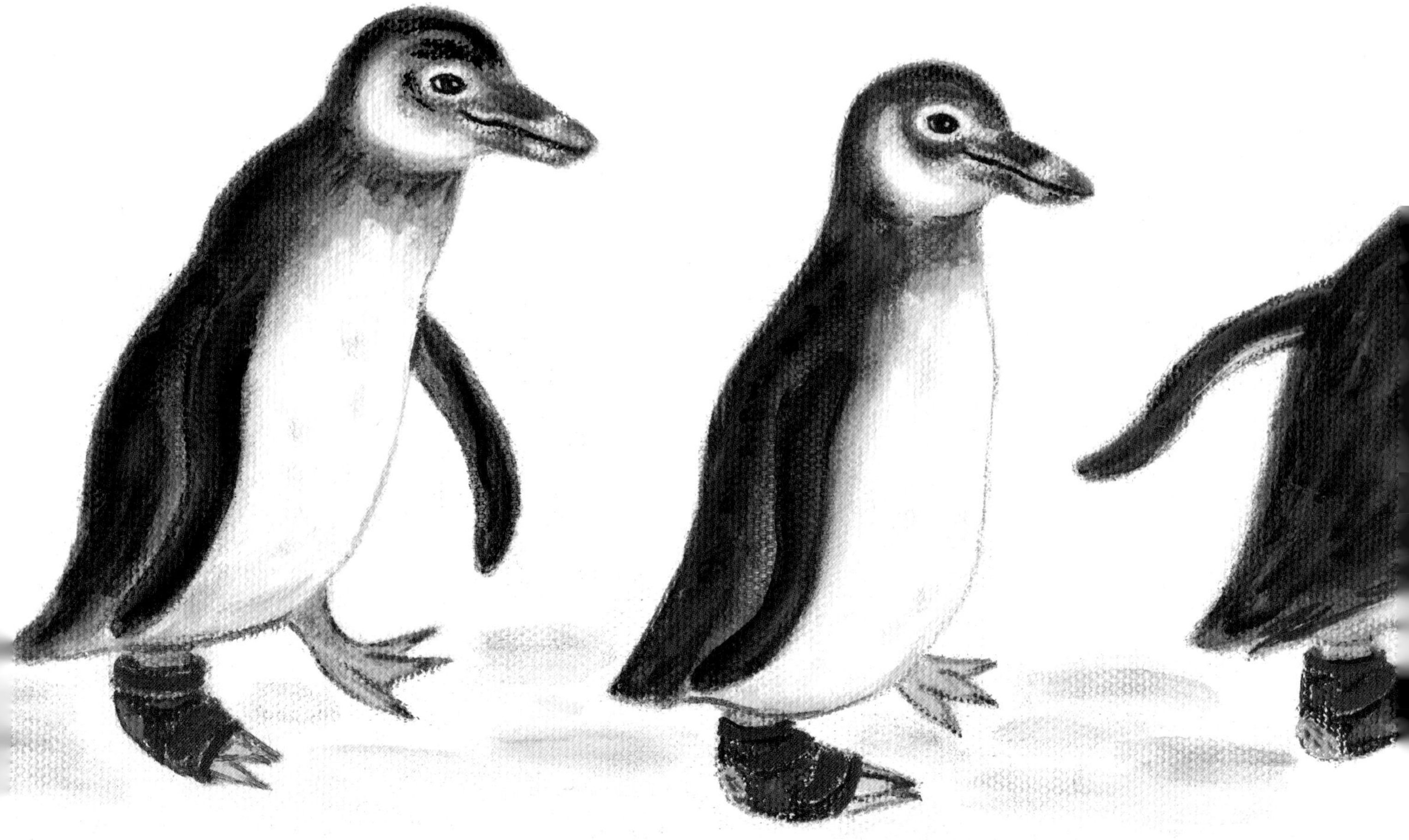

Lucky took off!

He walked and walked and walked.

He waddled all around the yard.

He hopped up and
down the rocks.

Rachel led him out to the pool. Only one
penguin paid any attention to Lucky's shoe.

He pecked it!

With a splash, Lucky jumped into the water.

"Hooray!" Rachel, the Zoo staff, the Teva people and everyone else clapped and cheered.

And, Lucky swam around
and around and around.

Lucky became famous...

From all over, children and parents came to see Lucky in his shoe.
Someone made a song and a video about him. Magazines and newspapers
published stories. He even appeared on television.

Lucky has shoes in many colors. He has special shoes for different holidays. Teva has promised to keep making shoes for Lucky all of his life.

That's how Lucky got his shoe…and his name, too!

Dictionary of Word Meanings

Burrow A hole or tunnel dug by a penguin using its feet. The penguin will lay its eggs in the burrow and live in it throughout the year.

Colony A group of penguins is a colony, a rookery or a waddle.

Coughing up half-digested fish The adult penguin will partially digest the fish they eat inside their stomachs. This usually takes several hours. When the food has been digested enough, the penguin coughs the food back up and feeds it to the chick by pouring the mixture into the chick's mouth.

Down Feathers Like all other birds, penguins have feathers. Penguin feathers are short, overlapping and densely packed. Down feathers are beneath this protective covering. They are light and fluffy and provide the insulation that penguins need to keep warm.

Hatchling A young animal that has recently emerged from its egg.

Humboldt Penguin A South American penguin that lives on the coast of Chile and Peru. Humboldt penguins swim in the cold water current which is named for the explorer, Alexander von Humboldt.

Infected When germs get inside your body, they might multiply and make you sick.

Joint A point where two bones in the body connect together.

Splint A rigid material used to support bones in order to hold them in place.

Teva A shoe company located near the Zoo that makes shoes and sandals out of materials that can be worn in the water (while hiking in creeks) and quickly dry out (to continue hiking on land).

Vulnerable Species An animal that is likely to become endangered (in danger of disappearing) unless what is threatening its survival and reproduction (ability to make babies) improve.

Photo: Dr. Marianna Favinsky

1: Lucky's Penguin Colony

2: Lucky swimming with his shoe.

3: Lucky and his shoe.

4: Lucky and his "birthday cake" made of fish frozen in colored ice with fish "frosting." Yummy!

Lucky

Lucky

lucky the penguin

Lucky

Luku the Penguin

Lucky

penguin

Lucky

Lucky

LUCKY

Lucky the Penguin

Mack

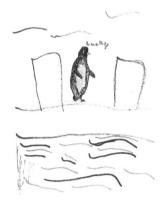

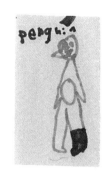

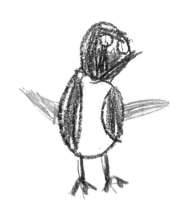

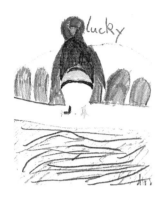

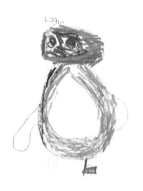

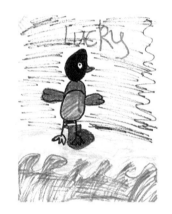

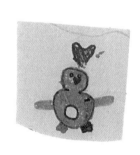

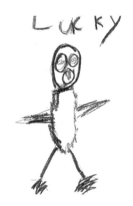

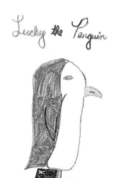

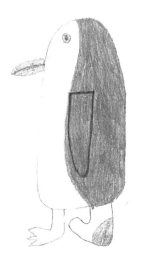

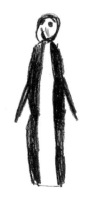

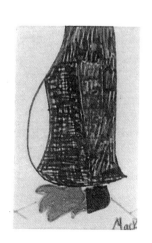